THE GREATEST GAME EVER PLAYED

A FOOTBALL STORY BY

PHIL BILDNER

ILLUSTRATED BY

ZACHARY PULLEN

PUFFIN BOOKS
An Imprint of Penguin Group (USA)

To Gersh and his dad,
to Turch and his dad.
—P.B.

To Hudson and all our future
Sundays and Monday nights.
—Z.P.

PUFFIN BOOKS
Published by the Penguin Group
Penguin Group (USA) LLC
375 Hudson Street
New York, New York 10014

USA * Canada * UK * Ireland * Australia
New Zealand * India * South Africa * China

penguin.com
A Penguin Random House Company

First published in the United States of America by G. P. Putnam's Sons,
a division of Penguin Young Readers Group, 2006.
Published by Puffin Books, an imprint of Penguin Young Readers Group, 2015.

Text copyright © 2006 by Phil Bildner.
Illustrations copyright © 2006 by Zachary Pullen.

THE LIBRARY OF CONGRESS HAS CATALOGED THE G. P. PUTNAM'S SONS EDITION AS FOLLOWS:
Bildner, Phil.
The greatest game ever played : a football story / by Phil Bildner ; illustrated by Zachary Pullen.
p. cm.
Summary: When their beloved baseball team, the New York Giants, moves to California, Sam and Pop switch
their loyalties to the other New York Giants and attend their championship game with the Baltimore Colts.
Includes historical note.
ISBN 978-0-399-24171-0 (hc)
[1. Football—Fiction. 2. Fathers and sons—Fiction.] I. Pullen, Zachary, ill. II. Title.
PZ7.B4923Gre 2006   [E]—dc22   2005025177

Puffin Books ISBN 978-0-14-751451-6

Manufactured in China

1 3 5 7 9 10 8 6 4 2

It's called the greatest game ever played.
The NFL Championship Game between the
Baltimore Colts and the New York Giants.
Yep, the greatest game ever played—
and in my mind, there's no doubt about it.

Before that game, it was all about baseball here in the city. And for me and Pop, it was all about our New York Giants.

At the Polo Grounds, during every seventh inning stretch, Pop would stand in the aisle and wind up like the great Sal Maglie.

"They call him 'The Barber' 'cause he likes to pitch batters in real close. Like he's shaving their chins. I tell ya, he owns the inside of the plate. That's what makes him so good."

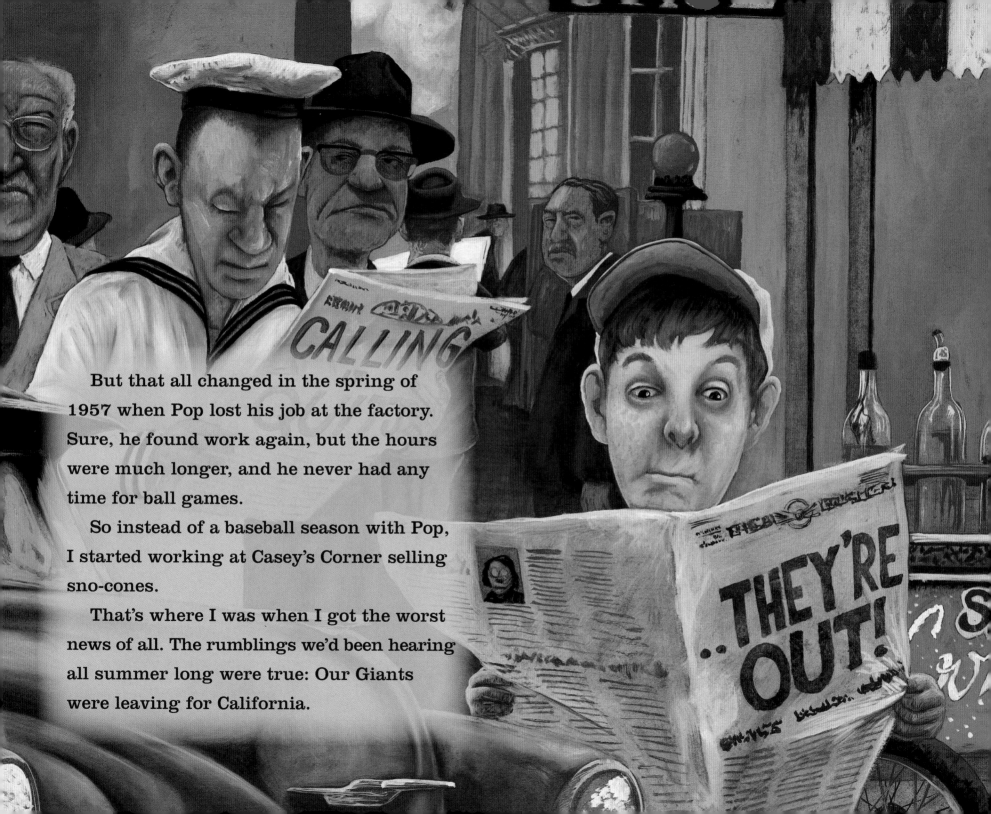

But that all changed in the spring of 1957 when Pop lost his job at the factory. Sure, he found work again, but the hours were much longer, and he never had any time for ball games.

So instead of a baseball season with Pop, I started working at Casey's Corner selling sno-cones.

That's where I was when I got the worst news of all. The rumblings we'd been hearing all summer long were true: Our Giants were leaving for California.

Moms tried to comfort us. "There's still the Yankees."

The Yankees? We *hated* the Yankees. No true Giants
fan could *ever* root for the Bronx Bombers!

"I tell ya, I'm through with baseball," Pop declared.

"I'll never go to a baseball game at Yankee Stadium."

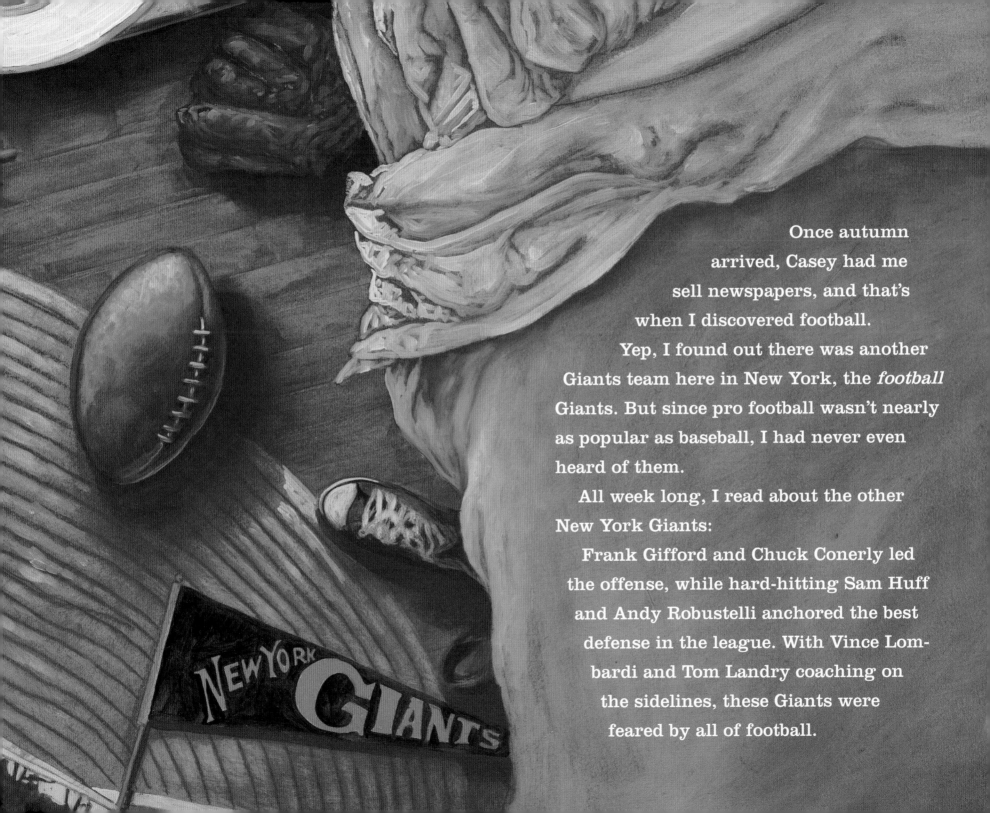

Once autumn arrived, Casey had me sell newspapers, and that's when I discovered football.

Yep, I found out there was another Giants team here in New York, the *football* Giants. But since pro football wasn't nearly as popular as baseball, I had never even heard of them.

All week long, I read about the other New York Giants:

Frank Gifford and Chuck Conerly led the offense, while hard-hitting Sam Huff and Andy Robustelli anchored the best defense in the league. With Vince Lombardi and Tom Landry coaching on the sidelines, these Giants were feared by all of football.

Every Sunday afternoon, I tuned to their games on WMGM radio. I tried to get Pop to listen, but he never showed much interest.

"I tell ya, the only Giants I'll listen to now play 3,000 miles from here," he said. "And since they're not about to move back, I'm not about to listen."

Well, a few days before Christmas, I lost *my* job.

"I feel just awful, Sam, but here's what I'm gonna do,"
Casey said. "An ol' buddy gave me a couple tickets to
Sunday's game. You go on and have 'em. Take a friend.
Take your dad."

Pop wanted no part of those tickets.

"I said I'd never go to a game at Yankee Stadium!" he snapped.
"And I meant it!"

Moms turned to Pop and gave him a look that only Moms could give.

"You said you'd never go to a *baseball* game at Yankee Stadium."

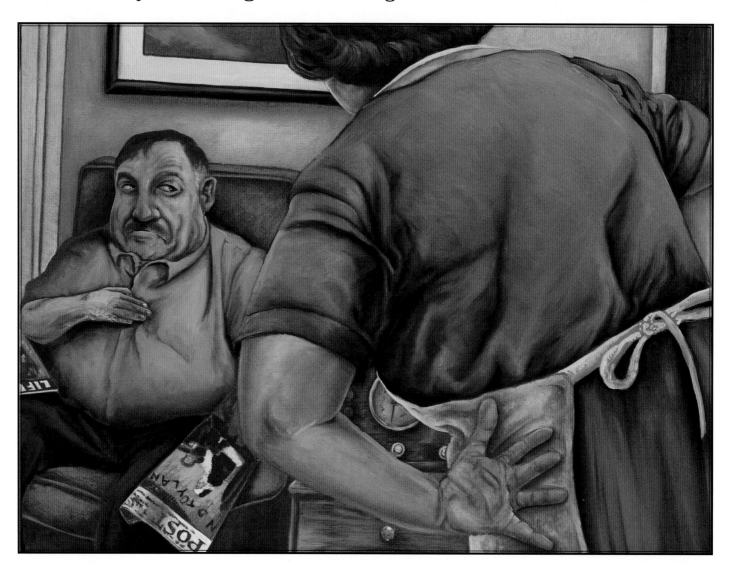

That Sunday after Christmas was raw and frigid, and Pop didn't say much on the subway ride over.

So I rambled on and on about the Colts:

"Their quarterback, Johnny Unitas, has the best arm in football, and they call their running back 'The Horse' because of the way he bobs his head and charges straight-on, and Raymond Berry led the league in catches, and then . . ."

I don't think Pop heard a word I was saying.

As soon as we stepped off the train at Yankee Stadium, all I could feel was the electricity in the air. All Pop *couldn't* feel were his fingers and toes, numbed by the bitter cold.

BALL GAME

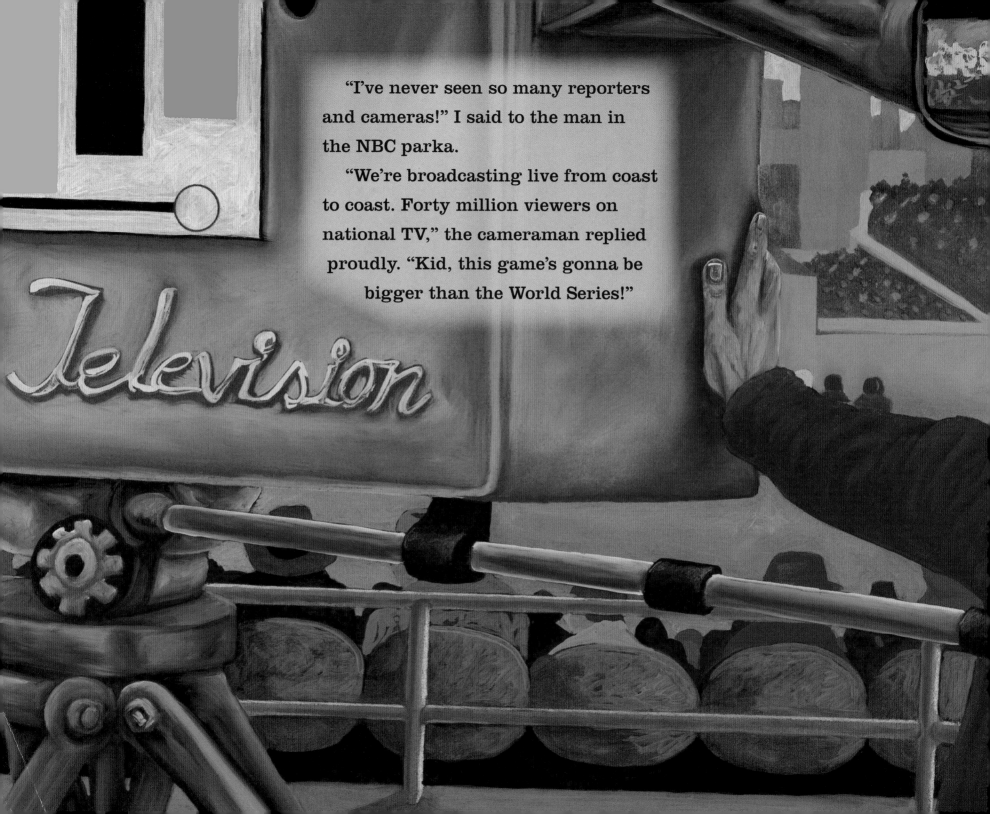

"I've never seen so many reporters and cameras!" I said to the man in the NBC parka.

"We're broadcasting live from coast to coast. Forty million viewers on national TV," the cameraman replied proudly. "Kid, this game's gonna be bigger than the World Series!"

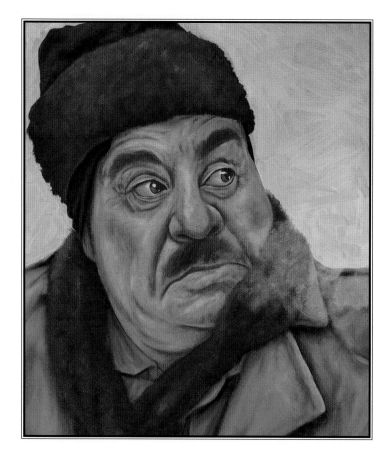

Once the game started, the
Giants couldn't hold on to the ball,
but neither could the Colts. In the
first quarter alone, the great
Johnny Unitas fumbled *and* threw
an interception.

"You dragged me to this?"
Pop grunted.

But Johnny U quickly found his game, and soon he was slinging and slashing his Colts downfield.

"Dee-fense!" I cried along with the crowd as the Colts set up to kick a field goal.

I peeked over at Pop. He was sitting up a little taller.

"Dee-fense!"

Sam Huff answered our calls.
He burst through the line
and blocked the kick!

The fans went wild, and even Pop stood up.

"I tell ya, this Giant defense may be the best there is," he said.

How did *he* know?

Well, that block woke our sleeping Giants. Frank Gifford
took off on a long run, and moments later, Pat Summerall,
the kicker born with a backwards right foot, kicked us a
field goal!

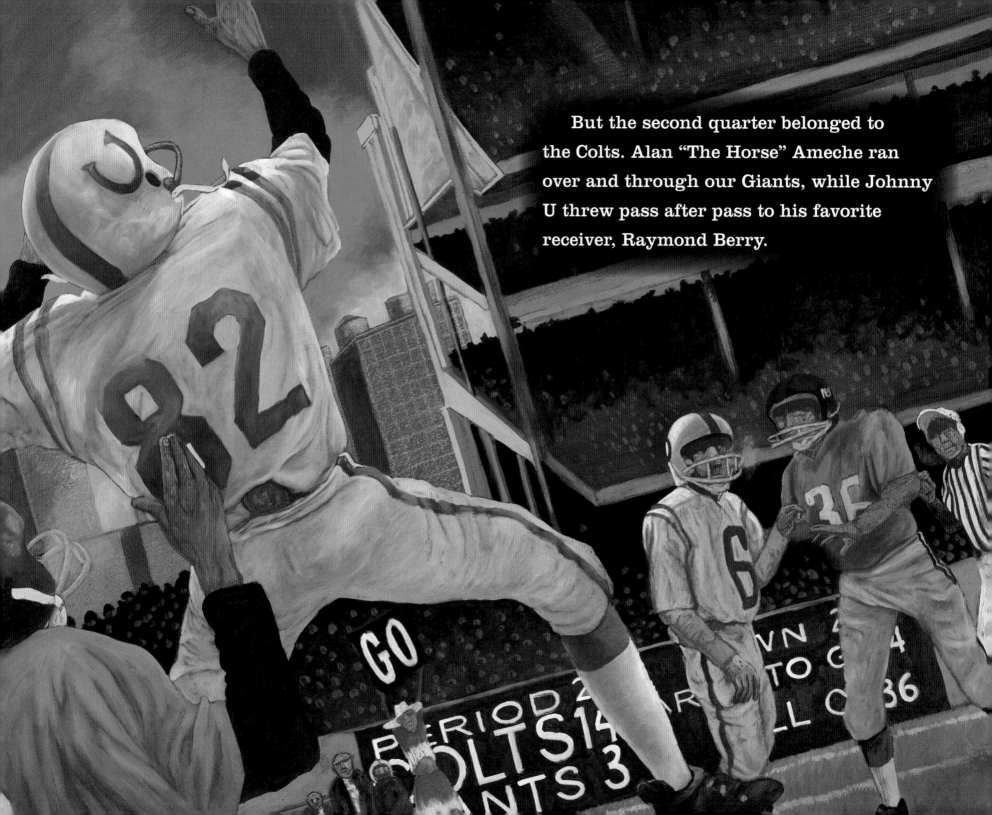

But the second quarter belonged to the Colts. Alan "The Horse" Ameche ran over and through our Giants, while Johnny U threw pass after pass to his favorite receiver, Raymond Berry.

"I tell ya, Sam, things might not look too good, but don't lose hope," Pop said. "With guys like Huff, Robustelli and 'Little Mo' Modzelewski, this Giant defense can hold its own against anyone."

"You *were* listening!" I exclaimed. "You were listening to the games all season!"

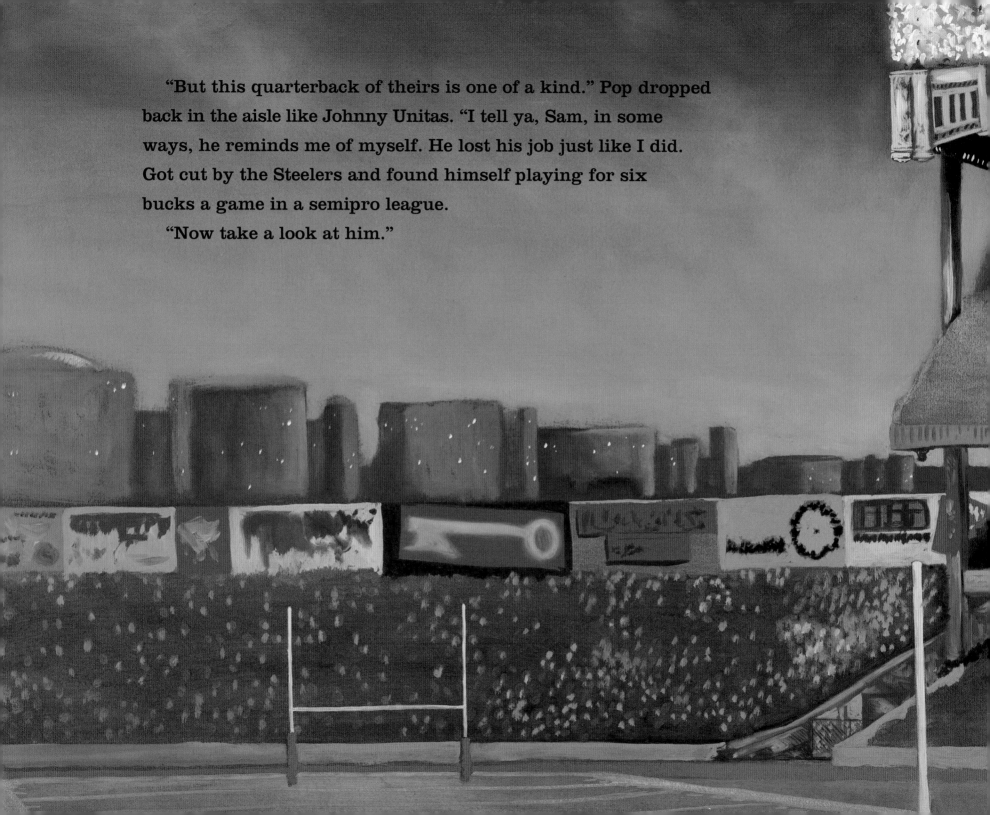

"But this quarterback of theirs is one of a kind." Pop dropped back in the aisle like Johnny Unitas. "I tell ya, Sam, in some ways, he reminds me of myself. He lost his job just like I did. Got cut by the Steelers and found himself playing for six bucks a game in a semipro league.

"Now take a look at him."

Back and forth
the teams battled.

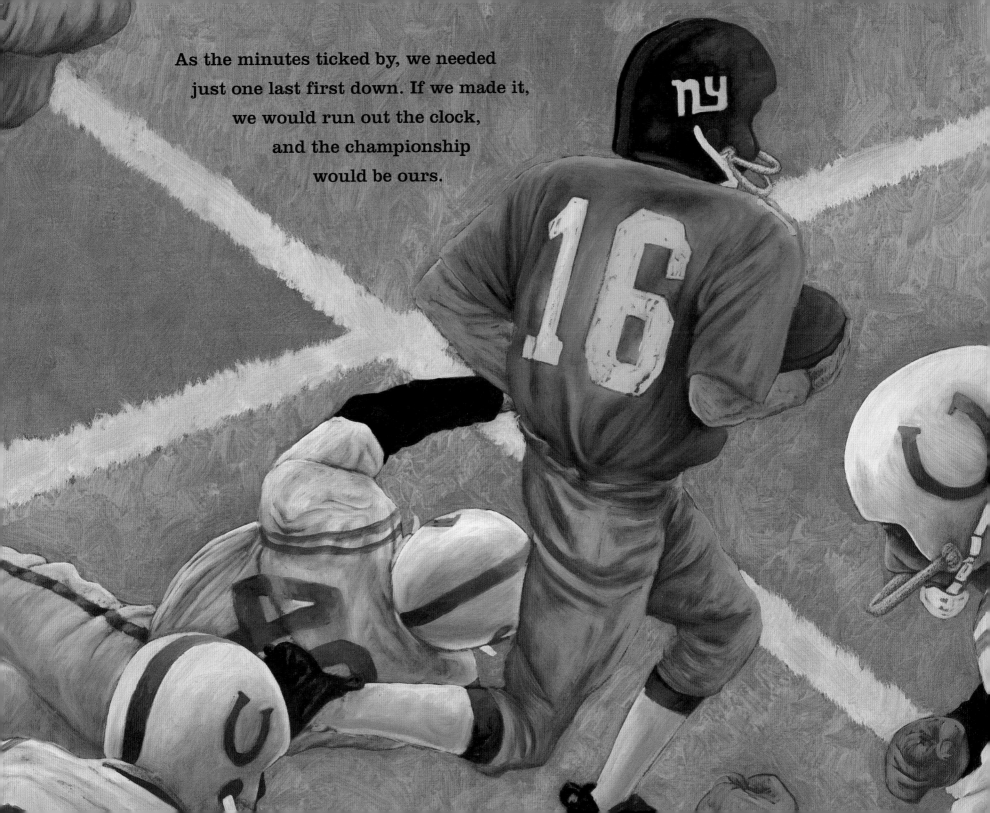

As the minutes ticked by, we needed
just one last first down. If we made it,
we would run out the clock,
and the championship
would be ours.

The Giants handed off to Gifford. He charged forward. Did he make it? **NO!**

Now Johnny U went to work. Once again, he looked to his favorite target, Raymond Berry. A 25-yard pass, a 15-yard pass, a 22-yard pass—it was like the two superstars were playing catch!

"Dee-fense!" Pop and I cried along with the crowd. "Dee-fense!"

But this time, our calls *weren't* answered. With seven ticks left on the clock, the Colts tied the game.

For the first time in NFL history, a game would be decided by sudden-death overtime. Whoever scored first would win the championship.

The stadium shook. The rafters
rattled. The crowd grew so loud,
Pop and I had to cover our ears!

The Giants got the ball first,
but just like at the start of the
game, that Colt defense held firm.
As we spilled from the stands
with the rest of the fans, Pop and
I looked at each other and groaned.
"Here comes Johnny U!"

Yep, the greatest game ever played—and in my mind, there's no doubt about it.

AFTERWORD

Pro football was a different game when the Baltimore Colts faced off against the New York Giants for the National Football League (NFL) championship on December 28, 1958. The nation was only first beginning to pay attention to the pro sport. Back then, the college game satisfied fans' football fancy, and when fans wanted to watch a professional sport, they turned to the national pastime, baseball.

That all changed as a result of the "Greatest Game Ever Played." On that Sunday afternoon, 40 million viewers (the largest-ever national television audience, to that point) watched the first and still the only NFL championship decided in sudden-death overtime.

Football fans everywhere reacted to this epic contest with the same overwhelming enthusiasm. The following season, more fans than ever tuned in to professional football. Executives from the still-developing television networks were quick to capitalize on what a nation had discovered, entering into a multimillion-dollar television contract for regular season games. Less than a decade later, the Super Bowl was born.

It's no coincidence that many of the key participants in the "Greatest Game Ever Played" were the ones who helped to transform football into the most popular television sport of the second half of the twentieth century. Of course, the game marked the birth of the legend of Johnny Unitas. It also featured hard-hitting linebacker Sam Huff, larger-than-life defensive tackle Art Donovan, and the great halfback Lenny Moore—all of whom became household names after that day. All in all, twelve future Pro Football Hall of Famers played at Yankee Stadium that afternoon.

It's also no coincidence that the key sideline participants would later help to transform the Super Bowl into the greatest single-day made-for-television sporting event. Weeb Ewbank, the Colts' head coach, would lead the New York Jets to victory in Super Bowl III in perhaps the greatest upset in sports history. Tom Landry, the Giants' defensive coach, would become head coach of the great Dallas Cowboy teams that earned the label "America's Team" in the 1970s and 1980s. And Vince Lombardi—well, after leading his Green Bay Packers to the first Super Bowl titles, they named the championship trophy after him.

For a game that meant so much to the NFL, it's amazing to consider how many people *didn't* see the "Greatest Game Ever Played." Because of local television rules, the game was blacked out in New York City, and the only New Yorkers able to see the game live had to have been there! Fans in Baltimore almost missed their team's defining moment too. During the Colts' final drive in overtime, the game was knocked off the air in Baltimore. Luckily, a time-out was called, and the technical difficulty was repaired just in time for Alan Ameche's championship-winning plunge into the end zone.

And the rest, as they say, is history.

PHIL BILDNER's first picture book, *Shoeless Joe & Black Betsy*, about baseball legend Shoeless Joe Jackson, won the Texas Bluebonnet Award. Since then he has written several more picture books about sports, including *The Shot Heard 'Round the World* and *The Turkey Bowl*. Phil lives in Brooklyn, New York, and you can visit him at **www.philbildner.com**.

ZACHARY PULLEN's humorous caricatures have been seen in dozens of publications, including *The New York Times Book Review* and *Sports Illustrated*. His first picture book, *The Toughest Cowboy*, received a starred review in *School Library Journal*, stating "Tall tales this enjoyable are hard to find." You can see more of Zak's artwork at **www.zacharypullen.com**.

A FACE-OFF BETWEEN LEGENDS, HISTORY IN THE MAKING, AND THE FATHER AND SON WHO BECOME PART OF IT ALL.

When the New York Giants move to San Francisco, Sam doesn't just lose his team—he loses the special time he had cheering them on with Pop. Then Sam discovers the *other* Giants—the football Giants. And when the Giants play the Baltimore Colts for the NFL championship, Sam drags a reluctant Pop along.

But can the Giants hold off the fearsome Colts, led by the legendary Johnny Unitas, and win the greatest game ever played?

"A great book for fathers to share with their kids."
—*Children's Literature*

INCLUDES HISTORICAL NOTES ON THE IMPACT OF THE GREATEST GAME

OTHER BOOKS BY PHIL BILDNER

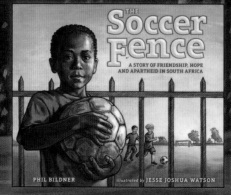

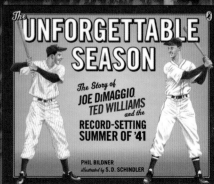

PUFFIN BOOKS
www.penguin.com/youngreaders

U.S.A. $8.99 / CAN. $9.99
Ages 5 to 8

ISBN 978-0-14-751451-6

EAN

9 780147 514516

50899

Sure enough, he led the Colts all the way to the Giants' one-yard line.

It all came down to this. Would our Giants be able to fight them

off one more time?

Unitas handed off to "The Horse." He lowered his bobbing head and plunged toward the end zone.

Did he make it?

TOUCHDOWN!
Our Giants had *lost*.

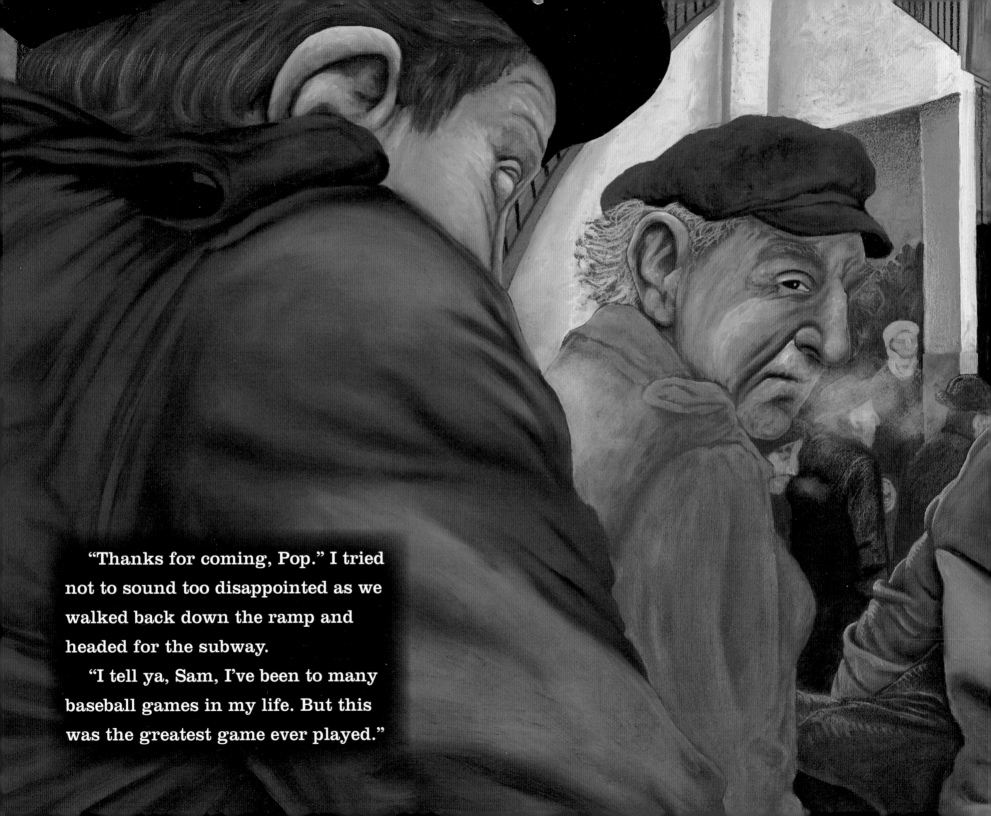

"Thanks for coming, Pop." I tried not to sound too disappointed as we walked back down the ramp and headed for the subway.

"I tell ya, Sam, I've been to many baseball games in my life. But this was the greatest game ever played."